READY TO GO!

adapted by Alex Harvey
based on the screenplay *"¡Vacaciones!"* by Brian J. Bromberg
illustrated by Art Mawhinney

Ready-to-Read

Simon Spotlight/Nickelodeon
New York   London   Toronto   Sydney   New Delhi

Based on the TV series *Dora the Explorer*™ and *Go, Diego, Go!*™ as seen on Nick Jr.™

SIMON SPOTLIGHT/NICKELODEON
An imprint of Simon & Schuster Children's Publishing Division
1230 Avenue of the Americas, New York, New York 10020
For information about special discounts for bulk purchases,
please contact Simon & Schuster Special Sales at 1-866-506-1949 or business@simonandschuster.com.
Manufactured in the United States of America 0312 LAK
First Edition
2 4 6 8 10 9 7 5 3 1
ISBN 978-1-4424-3538-4

Dora and Boots are going camping with Diego and Baby Jaguar.

They packed their camping snacks, two sleeping bags, two water bottles, a flashlight, and binoculars.

☑  Snacks

☑ Sleeping bags

☑  Water bottles

☑ Flashlight

☑  Binoculars

To get to Diego and Baby Jaguar, Map says Dora and Boots need to go through the Nutty Forest and Isa's Garden.

Look! There are Tico
and Benny.
They are going on a trip
too!

Benny says, "For our beach trip, we need bathing suits, towels, a blanket, and a surfboard."

Do you see what else
Benny and Tico need?
Sunscreen!

- ☑ Bathing suits
- ☑ Towels
- ☑ Blanket
- ☑ Surfboard
- ☑ Sunscreen

Now Tico and Benny are
ready!

Tico gives Dora and Boots a ride through the Nutty Forest. But Tico's car stops!

Tico's Nutty Car runs on
nuts.
And they are almost all
gone!

"The car will not go without nuts," Benny says. Tico fills his car with nuts from the Nutty Forest.

"Yum, yum," says the Nutty Car. Soon the Nutty Car is full of nuts and ready to go!

Tico drops us off
at Isa's Garden.

Isa is going on a trip too.

"I am going to ski at Snowy
Mountain," says Isa.

Isa has packed her skis,
her ski poles,
goggles, and a scarf.
But she is missing her
helmet. Do you see it?

"Ah, there it is," Isa says.
"Thank you. Now I am
ready."

☑ Skis

☑ Poles

☑ Goggles

☑ Scarf

☑ Helmet

Isa heads off to Snowy Mountain.

Now Dora and Boots can go meet Diego and Baby Jaguar.

They made it to the
rainforest!
What's that sound?
Chhh . . . chhh . . . chhh.

"Hey, that log is moving,"
Boots says.
Who is inside that log?

It is Swiper! Swiper grabs their camping snacks and throws them into the river!

Just then Diego and Baby
Jaguar appear in a canoe.
"Swiper took our snacks,"
Boots tells them.

"Come on," says Diego. "We can go down the river in my canoe."

They paddle fast.
Baby Jaguar grabs the
snacks out of the water!

That night Dora, Diego, Boots, and Baby Jaguar sit around the campfire.

What a great camping trip!